Chicka
Chicka

For Rick Selvaggi—B. M.
For Leslie Pinkham—M. S.
For Libby and Liza, Helen
and Morris—L. E.

Thanks to Lisa van Drasek.

ISBN 0-439-73108-9

Text copyright © 2004
by Bill Martin Jr and
Michael Sampson.
Illustrations copyright
© 2004 by Lois Ehlert.
All rights reserved.
Published by
Scholastic Inc.,
557 Broadway,
New York,
NY 10012,

1·2·3

Bill Martin Jr
Michael Sampson
Lois Ehlert

SCHOLASTIC INC.
New York   Toronto   London   Auckland   Sydney
Mexico City   New Delhi   Hong Kong   Buenos Aires

by arrangement with Simon & Schuster Books for
Young Readers, Simon & Schuster Children's
Publishing Division. SCHOLASTIC and associated
logos are trademarks and/or registered trademarks
of Scholastic Inc.

12 11 10 9 8 7 6 5 4 3 2 1   5 6 7 8 9 10/0

Printed in Singapore   46

First Scholastic printing, January 2005

This work is based on *Chicka Chicka
Boom Boom*, written by Bill Martin Jr
and John Archambault and illustrated
by Lois Ehlert.

The text for this book is
set in Bembo.

The illustrations for this
book are rendered in cut
Pantone-coated papers.

1 told **2**
and **2** told **3,**
"I'll race you to the top
of the apple tree."

"Climb," said **4**
   to **5** and **6,**
   bright little numbers
   that join the mix.

"Hurry!" yelled **7**
   to number **8,**
   slow-poke fellow
   who's always late.

"Chicka Chicka
1, 2, 3 . . .
Will there be a
place for me?"

Here comes **9**
to the apple tree.
Next comes **10**
and then **11**.
"Wow, these apples
taste like heaven!"

"Chicka Chicka
1, 2, 3 . . .
Will there be a
place for me?"

Hot pink **12,**
lucky **13,**
picking apples
red and green.

14, 15 . . .
Can't you see?
They all want to climb
the apple tree.

"Chicka Chicka
1, 2, 3 . . .
Will there be a
place for me?"

16's next
to make the scene,
climbing branches
with **17**.

18, 19,
one more's **20**.
Numbers, numbers,
there are plenty.

"Chicka Chicka
1, 2, 3 . . .
Will there be a
place for me?"

20.0

Curvy **30,**
flat-foot **40**
climbing up
to join the party!

50's fine
and **60**'s dandy.
70's hair
is long and sandy.

"Chicka Chicka
1, 2, 3 . . .
Will there be a
place for me?"

"Let's climb more,"
says treetop **80,**
higher and higher,
up to **90,**

until at last there's **99,**
and all the numbers
are feeling fine,

except for **0,**
who begins to cry.

"Chicka Chicka
1, 2, 3 . . .
Will there be a
place for me?"

Oh, no!

Buzzing close!
Bumblebees!

0 hides
behind the tree.

"GET OUT OF OUR TREE!"
the bumblebees shout,
and all the numbers
tumble out.

90, 80,
70 fall,
hit the ground
in a free-for-all.

60, 50,
40 run.
No more climbing,
no more fun!

30 next,
then sweet little **20**.
Numbers, numbers,
no longer plenty!

19 and **18,**
my, oh my!
Frightened numbers
jump and fly!

17, 16,
15 more.
Now **14** has hit the
floor.

And **13,** too—
unlucky guy!
12 had almost
touched the sky!

Bent-up **11**.
(Wait! Where's **10**?)
9, 8, 7
follow then.

Twisted **6**
and top-hat **5**,
4, 3, 2, 1
take a dive!

"Chicka Chicka
1, 2, 3 . . .
Now I know
the place for me!"

0 leaps into the sky.
Brave little number,
he's not shy.

0 lands on top
of the tree,
joins with **10**.
Now **100** you see!

10

"Chicka Chicka
1, 2, 3 . . .
Here's the place
that's just for me!"

All the numbers
come back out,
higher and higher,
as they shout . . .